T0207696

LOTTERY LOSER,
YOU ONLY LIVE TWICE

BRENDA LEE BURKE

Order this book online at www.trafford.com
or email orders@trafford.com

Most Trafford titles are also available at major online book retailers.

Print information available on the last page.

ISBN: 978-1-6987-1126-3 (sc)
ISBN: 978-1-6987-1125-6 (e)

Library of Congress Control Number: 2022903710

Trafford rev. 02/25/2022

 www.trafford.com

North America & international
toll-free: 844-688-6899 (USA & Canada)
fax: 812 355 4082

DEATH TRIP

SUMMER 2050

What would you do with a million dollars?

I'd build a go-cart track right in my own backyard!

Chip's heart pounds the pavement in time to his feet as they stomp through dark puddles, sloshing cold water up his heavy, drenched jeans, some of the spray getting his face and streaming down his neck, snaking its way to his heaving chest.

A glance back reveals a horrifying picture bopping up and down like a shaky recording—three men coming at him, slapping the road with soaked shoes, wet leather clinging to them like second skins.

Uneven and slippery, the cobblestones up ahead will make for a tricky escape, but Chip has traveled enough to know precisely where to place his feet. On the move across Europe and its well-laid culture and even in the flurry of running for his death, he recalls his study of many a platform heel, how the wearer, mostly male now, steps firmly atop the integrated stones of many shapes rather than gingerly sliding off the sides. And looking uncool.

The surrounding shopping district is abandoned, illuminated only by streetlights appearing as ancient as some of their neighboring buildings. Tiny high-end shops squeeze together to boast the world's finest dog-skins in Black Obsession, Rich Chocolate, and Townie Tawny. Hovering about a foot off the floor, faceless floating mannequins sport the pieced-together leathers in soul-defining seriousness. Refined, sleek, and unadorned. Safe, minimalist '90s have not gone out of style, even sixty years later.

Darkened cafes slumber, unaware of rain and running men and unapologetic for their empty, lonely patios with chairs stacked inside hours ago, the smiles and relaxed chattering of patrons reduced to an echo of earlier daylight.

A cat scurries behind a stone wall of an old church standing statuesque and tall, menacing and overbearing, hints of musty Vatican beauty gracing its stone-heavy facade.

Spotting the cat, Chip thinks of Jewels, the wise, soft-eyed Siamese of his childhood. She knew too much, and if she could tell the globe how to save itself, Chip knows in his heart it would be possible.

In his frantic running state, he finds his mind flashing to the world's current no-pet policy. Permanent strays fed by anyone and their sister, praying for good health and survival in wake of a global shortage of the domestic veterinarian.

One of the rain-slicked male chasers raises his smooth air Taser, and Chip feels fire slice into his flesh. He sinks back to a November day with CoCo by the makeshift winter camp, snuggling under a frostbitten wool blanket. Her veins are liquid fire. Up in the mountains, that's where he wants to go now. He can smell the snow, taste her warmth.

Another electric crack deafens the air, and Chip looks down, sees himself staggering, dragging his legs under a chain-link fence, dreams his body huddled on the concrete stairs leading down to the cat's church basement. Cold is the only sound.

Sifting back to the camp with CoCo, giant, fluffy snowflakes whip all around him, the wind shrieks through the trees, and the sky is wild. She rests her head on his chest and pulls into him. He floats away, snow tickling his forehead, melting, flowing down his face like tears. His core is thick with hotness, a pushing weight that lifts only when he sees white.

TAKE THIS JOB

SUMMER 2045

As he lies bleeding on the church steps, spinning somewhere between near-death and reality, Chip remembers winning the biggest lottery in history.

First, he does what every Tom, Dick, and Gizelda says they'll do if they ever win it big. He quits his job.

On his last day at MechTech, the copier hums out copy after copy of retro tech copy, and he snatches each page as it spits out of the machine. *Cha-chung, cha-chung* . . . same-old, same-old. Inexperienced characters at the office encourage Chip to make the copies via the old style . . . a new marketing gimmick.

Too weak to will his thoughts elsewhere, unable to change the scene, and too tired to care, he's compelled to follow the daily thread of his working existence. Like the draggy appeal of an old movie, the familiarity comforts him, while the repetition haunts him, burning out a small corner of his brain.

Humming along, just like the copier, no end in hearing range, no beginning . . . just like his life memories. Technically speaking, his job is important to certain people. They need their tech copy. On time. In proper format. Including matter-of-fact descriptions of how to reboot your Taser, practice your float skills, or maximize your PalmTech.

And hand care is complicated these days. If you want to survive, you quickly learn the rule of pinky and hire yourself a licensed hand magician who makes a hefty bit by tuning and repairing intricate wirings within your right hand, being extra careful not to damage any wires connected directly to your left brain.

Hand managers care for the epidermis of the right hand, taking manicures to the next level. Nails are kept super short so as not to interfere with the way they tap the palm to send messages. Skin must be protected from the burning sun (usually, with the help of breathable, anti-fry gloves). Right hands are also to be massaged regularly to ensure dexterity and joint health. Arthritis simply ejects you from the communications game.

What Chip really wants to do (and what nearly all technical writers really want to do) is dream up fiction. All of it a fantasy with no time nor sense, except his own and whatever he thinks will compel the reader, *his* reader.

Along the side of his sagging, working-drone mind, he brews up a book. One good book about superbugs. He plans to spring it off the latest Ebola wipeout, bringing in a few crazy characters and peppering it with drama. Then he'll tie it all up with a pinch of sarcasm, whip it good with wacky humor. Hell, even if it takes him ten years of brain whispering . . . Besides, hasn't his boring job put him in a coma for at least that long?

Yes, on his last day at MechTech, as he dreams of his great fiction-to-be, the grating sound of someone clearing their throat brings him smashing back to real life. The boss, that wretched rack of bones, his ugly mug appearing on Chip's brain screen.

His name is Dan Sanders, a.k.a. Sandy Paper. He even has sandy-colored hair, which is even more annoying. Doesn't the man realize he could choose any color in the world? Why pick bland blond? The overrated obsession with the color faded years ago, sparkling silver taking its place as the world's number one choice.

Sandy's smile is the worst, radiating from a person who truly believes he's better than most, someone with no idea that perhaps all people are equal, that a bum on the street is just as important as any rich dude.

"How's the Roberts file coming along?" barks Sandy, a poor attempt at office casual. Chip drifts. He'd rather think about his main *Secret Superbugz* character, Bradley Bowman, blowing his nose.

After crumpling the tissue into an uneven ball and hiding the boogers safely within its soft folds, Bradley Bowman sits down and begins to type.

Meanwhile, Sandy, definitely very old school, is having a problem being part of management. Act too lenient, they walk all over you; too strict, they hate your lungs—an issue as old as the fields. He considers Chip a real work of music because he will "Yes, right away!" to your face, but you get the feeling he's smirking on the inside and ready to put a tack—no, twenty tacks—on your chair (Do tacks still exist? Probably deemed redundant like the penny and the paper clip.)

Sandy secretly wishes for the bad old days of sixty-hour-plus work weeks, networking, gossip by the water cooler. New government mandates based on an old Sweden model dictate that nobody can work more than ten hours a week. All wages are automatically doubled to compensate for the financial fall-out. Apparently, lottery ticket sales generate the rest of the compensation.

Sandy scratches his head. He fully understands the need for leisure in lives. But why outlaw networking and gossip? In his view, those two things are a complete necessity, especially with the banning of retirement.

After his two hours of work that day, Chip takes five steps to get to his office door, nineteen steps to get to the elevator, and exactly seventy-seven steps to get to his car in float parking. He opens the car door as he always does, pushes the float button, and takes his routine nap while floating home. As he closes his eyes, he thanks Odama for saving the world back in 2020 when he secretly pulled some strings to halt the ongoing crisis involving Israel, thereby preventing a global nuclear attack. (Nobody seemed to notice in a time when very few could see beyond their own face mask.)

Because of one man's actions in saving the planet, Chip is currently able to take full advantage of C2C (car-to-car) technology. Perfected by 2030, it leads to the end of conscious driving as he knows it. Ah, he can finally just lay back and . . . He doesn't see it, but the city he floats through is breathtaking, all stretched-up buildings built with layers of concrete. His dad says the Jetsons' world has become a reality, whatever that means. The last of city green ran out ten years ago, along with the domestic family doctor.

At home that night, Chip zaps in his lucky lottery numbers. Exactly twenty minutes later comes the message: *You've won! The jackpot.*

That night he quits his job. He doesn't actually even bother to quit, just doesn't log on his float screen to finalize the deed. He books the first rocket to GodKnowsNotWhere where he'll have time to think of what to do with the money. It's an outdated hobby, but soaking up the sun is something he still relishes, even after new fry warnings.

During the twenty-minute flight, he sits, balding head spinning with delirium. He can feel his bare scalp skin against the craft's cat-skin seat and prays the rest of his hair will finally fall out. This will save him from zapping it off to impress future employers and, of course, the guys.

He goes zoom-class everything and sits back, feeling like the richest man on Mars. Immediately after reaching GodKnowsNotWhere, he perches motionless on the same beach day after day in nothing but the same red anti-fry suit, the sun eventually searing through the garment's protective barrier, making his skin shrink and blister, his lips cracking beneath his new lip shield, a parma-grin tugging at whisker-speckled corners. Just beyond the reddish haze of his eyelids, he hears a gentle motion of turquoise waters, yawns at the image of yellow bikinis tied predictably to same-rounded hips, feels scorching sand beneath his own sagging, sinking buttocks.

Let everyone wonder where he is. He's rich!

As he dreams blood dreams, waiting to die, Chip knows why the Win guys are chasing him—mostly to lop off his right hand and access his codes and, therefore, his cash, assets, and identity.

A meeting, a meeting, it's all explained at that meeting . . .

PALMS UP

"I'll put this as simply as I can. Embedded in the right palm is a complex network of electronics leading up the arm, through the shoulder and neck region and attaching itself, eventually, to part of the left brain," explains the man with old-style Giggle glasses to a room full of people interested in learning, firsthand, about this latest technology. All citizens over the age of fifteen are to receive this mandatory operation, which will obviously take numerous years to phase in.

"Will this replace round-screen TVs, skin phones, telepathic photos, all the old tech?" pipes a newbie reporter.

"You bet," assures the man, rubbing his palms together. "A mini screen in the left brain deciphers everything through the fingertips and even has the capability to respond. People will essentially tap their own palms to message, call, float, get info, anything."

A futurist raises his hand. "So the human body becomes an information entity in itself. But if we're essentially part robot," he wonders," how will the rest of our bodies continue to function?"

"Ah, good question," says Giggle, noticing all eyes are now on him and this burning piece of information he's about to impart. "Through an intricate surgery, everything is rewired to enable the right brain to take care of everything else that's human—thinking, vision, motor control—while the left brain is on standby to take commands from the user's fingerprints and reveal whatever information is needed . . . identification, banking, everything."

Then quickly answering their unasked question, "Because the 'computerized' left brain still has other biological functions to perform. Of course, it will continue to work with its sister brain. Like a true relationship, these two are inseparable at the core even though they seek their own 'careers.' Once a month or so, just like our modern-day marriage, they may invite a third party to join them for planned pleasure excursions to strengthen their bond and take their relationship to new heights . . ."

"Mars!" quips the newbie reporter who immediately retreats, blushing. But seconds later he's puzzled by how a "third party" will help the brains.

"Of course," replies Giggle, "in the realm of human sexuality . . . and relations, of course, this could open many, many doors to the future . . . as long as a potential damaging virus, of course, is kept in check."

In reaction to giggles and murmurs and a little bit of confusion, potential questions bubbling, the man presses his fingertips to either side of his forehead as if massaging his own brain to get back to his plane of thought. In his authoritative excitement, he has said too much.

"What we have done, ladies and cavemen, is traveled from the prehistoric paper society to one of total information integration. Entirely within the human body."

The deafening round of applause that follows burns in Chips ears as he silently sits and watches, an anxiousness growing up his legs and radiating his core until he becomes two with the feeling.

"My PalmTech." He whispers it, feels it tickle his tongue like a new dirty word. He stands stiffly, needing no introduction. Greeting him are rounds of cheering, shouting, clapping, whistling, and best of all, Mars invites from short athletic-breasted women ready to take him all in as the world's new genius inventor.

HACKERS ANONYMOUS

It doesn't take long to discover the only glitch in the hand-does-all technology. Even after a person leaves the Earth, their PalmTech lives on. It's still active—anyone can get access—any expert hacker, that is.

Hacking has been around forever and still no cure. Even old FakeBook is totally screwed because of hackers. Sheesh, it isn't *entirely* Chip's fault the multimillion brainstorm gets snatched from him, finds its way underground, lawsuits tunneling from all directions. It's supposed to be his ticket to financial freedom, similar to promises of lottery ads.

When Chip is ten, he sees his FakeBook idea as an innocent social network, but by the time he's seventeen, his invention is stolen by the lottery corp, which he comes to know later as Win, and that paves the way for future massive bank break-ins, celebrity assassinations, and worst of all, fake identities.

After answering an online ad calling for "fresh tech inventors," his FakeBook is born. Eager and inexperienced, he arrives at some clinical building downtown, entirely spills the corn about his gigantic idea, leaves with a glow-on, rubbing his palms together and dreaming of the cash to come his way, then is totally duped three months later when he sees some dark-suited man on the news taking credit for how *his* new social media will change the world.

It becomes a sour joke to him, the entire FakeBook rage. And at the height of online *friends*, Chip mourns for folks like twenty-two-year-old Tina Jackson from Texas who wakes up three minutes before her alarm on Tuesday, scratches her lower back (itchy because of tattoo poisoning), yawns, then types rapidly to tell the world about it. She even shares a recipe! Despite his food-trained tongue, recipes are on Chip's yuck list, right up there with churches and flipflops. He makes a mental note to add that to his multiple profiles.

At the time, like everyone and their mother, he can't help but seek attention online. Like millions of followers, he simply has a boring life and nothing to do. He hates himself for this and considers writing a book titled *Life Online*, about a man who spends so much of his time there he can no longer distinguish it from reality and even becomes a main character in his favorite cheesy game.

But now Chip's tired of the entire sleepy scene. He just wants to die and get on with his second life. A better life.

Why can't people just leave him the hell alone?

He knows PalmTech hasn't helped the information epidemic, although he means it as a high-tech way for people to have privacy and freedom. Instead, it tempts a supreme hacking of privacy and identity, the literal kind that has some desperate souls digging up graves and chopping off hands . . . mostly of the rich. The result? An instant life makeover. Just like the lottery promise.

HAPPILY NEVER AFTER

While Chip is busy winning the lottery, King Pong, head of the lottery corp (again, otherwise known as Win) emerges from his den.

"So who's the next loser in line?" A strapping old man at an enviable five feet, he peers up at his scrawny, less-fortunate assistant burdened by tallness.

"Chip Munk," replies Scrawny, stone faced.

"Mmm. His initiation set up? What's his profile?"

King considers tapping out his own palm research, but it's not easy for his small wrinkled hands. He quietly leaves the task to Scrawny who rapidly taps his palm and within seconds, has Chip's entire history under his powerful pinky.

"Um . . .," he reports. "Chip Munk . . . tizzy-headed, working android, plain fam from southwest . . . lucky enough to be sixty-five . . . in the old days would have been celebrating retirement . . . great pawn, a rough beauty she is, goes by CoCo Bean—and he's the best catch for her because he's into winning . . . winning anything by the looks of it."

"What proves that?" King strokes his bald chin.

"His dad ruled casino malls."

"Oh, so Chip was practically born on a poker table." Scrawny chuckles at the old phrase, while King continues his assessment.

"Ah, probably the result of good new-fashioned strip poker! Good, this one's easy as long as his sweet little CoCo Bean doesn't get in the way. Her humanitarian level?"

A few quick finger taps and then . . . "Die-hard anti-tech revolutionary. Squirms for the bad old days. Into caring for creatures . . . especially Chip," Scrawny adds with a smirk before exiting.

"Wait!" But Scrawny is gone, unable to work a minute more than his daily two hours. "Keep an ear on her," King slowly messages into his palm, his free hand itching a hard-to-reach spot just below his ribcage, which is trapped beneath his new spray-on shirt, and the more he rubs the fabric, the itchier the spot gets. "Damn palm crap! What the hell was wrong with keyboards anyway?"

In his coldening state, Chip drifts back to a knock at his door. Best Bud with another crazy, lucrative idea.

"Let's do FootBook to go along with your fancy-pants palm stuff," he snorts. "It's time FakeBook got a *real* friend!"

"Hell . . . maybe." In his happily-never-after way, he smiles for the first time in weeks. He's hooked on the latest version of Uboob at the moment, and this is just the ticket to get him off.

After an hour of exhausting, high-inspirational talk, Best leaves Chip's estate, passing a gigantic water fountain that trickles down on itself. That tinkling, gentle splashing sound, combined with his mounting excitement over his own ideas, encourages the sudden need to pee. He unzips beside the fountain, and they water the grass in unison.

Chip told them to shut that damn thing off. The water police will nab him again!

As he watches Best through the window, Chip looks to the right and sees the stray dogs, almost hears them munching the food he's left for them, swears they're whispering about him. Since cancer has been cured in canines only, the dog population has exploded. He really shouldn't be feeding them in culling season, but he feels sorry for them, remembers when they were beloved pets, not harvested for their skins.

He looks to the left and catches a glimpse of someone moving by the fence, stooped over, toe-to-head goth-black, stealthy, like a fashionable enemy.

The stranger hangs on the edge of his mind caught between waves of pain and an ocean of sweet death. The night is foggy, as murky as his thoughts, outlining tree branches blurred against time. A swift slicing sound, the deed done, the palm off in a bloody mess, holding the lock to his future.

He pictures the last time he should have seen CoCo. The private photograph reruns itself, forces its crisp image across his pinched temples, his body crumpled in the pool of church blood.

"No worries, folks," CoCo grins, wet ringlets of red sticking to her forehead in the hot breeze. "He'll be here. Any minute now." Her curls shake despite being weighed down with sweat as she nods a little too anxiously. She, of course, doesn't realize that along with the animals' help, she has enough good energy to save the world when she chooses to.

The man in the gray pinstriped suit taps the toe of his left shoe on the patch of pavement behind him as if to reposition his foot inside so that his toes are closer to the front.

Ah, more in control now.

The corners of his mouth turn down into a perma-pout as she appears to study something invisible beyond him. Rolling her eyes and silently fake-praying, she takes a deep breath and lets it escape in short puffs.

Frustration bubbles in her throat settles in her gut.

Later her new dark feelings will find themselves at their limits. She flashes forward a hundred years to her next lifetime to when she will still ache, still want him, still hate him.

"Could I get you a coffee . . . Miss Bean . . . ?" Pinstripe offers, looking a little too eager. He loves his Boobies coffee shops, they make the best java known to woman. She loves her name, the way it sounds, the way it feels on other people's tongues.

"Um no, thanks."

"Ah, a nonaddict . . . Better for ya." He nods, shifting his gaze to clouds passing overhead. "Stuff will drive ya crazy."

CoCo sighs and finds herself thinking about how popular suicide has become. Preventing someone from killing themselves is against the law now, thanks to the Second Chance Act. Ever since peoplekind have discovered reincarnation is real, and ever since they got breeze of how to tamper with the process, everyone wants out of their first life early so they can come back as their *dream self.* The trade-on is, of course, that when reincarnated folks live out their self-made destiny in their second lifetime, that's it, life on Earth is over for them. No third chances.

You only live twice.

As predicted, many dream of winning the lottery, and if they concentrate real hard just as they exit their first life, they actually do end up winning at some point in life number 2. It adds up to a lotta lotteries, and because the corporation is corrupt, it also means a lotta monies for those involved.

Chip plays the game, he thinks, to his advantage. His first life pegs him as a starving, homeless man, each day a street struggle. He does off himself (CoCo still isn't sure of his method) and plans for his better tomorrow. In his case, a lottery winner.

The only glitch? The reincarnated life can't entirely go as the person orders it. And it could happen completely out of context, which tends to mess things up. Someone could plan to win the lottery in their second life and then be killed and eaten by a hippo the next day. Fate still plays the most part. That means someone could live out most of their second life, their absolute last, before matters change according to their second-life plan.

CoCo remembers one enthusiastic lottery winner from a few months back. It's an elderly woman, frail and forgotten, living out her second life actually worse off than her first.

"I won this for my family so they can have better lives," she tells the radio the day she claims an obscene amount of lottery money. She, of course, had ordered this much-improved path of destiny on the deathbed of her first miserable life as a working drone. The last thought the dying becomes their reincarnated plan for their next life.

The day after she wins, the woman's hand is hacked off by a stranger and her identity stolen.

None of this makes much sense to CoCo, who would rather live out her present life to its potential than be surprised by who she comes back as for her *second chance.* She clings to her own time warp, devoting all energies to the "there and now."

Over all else, she values animals. They are her hope, her religion in a noisy, tilted world. She says a silent prayer for coffee zombies, poor souls who have drowned their brains in Boobies shops. She mutters indistinguishable garble about the equally-frustrating state of those hooked on zips, a scary combo of drugs (all are legalized at this point) to be absorbed through the fingertips. (A near cry from lowly cigarettes of the distant past.) Good old *Breaking Bad* on steroids, she muses.

Welcome to NuZoo reads the silly sign painted in white. *Who thought up that name anyway?* She shifts her weight from one foot to the other, tapping the side of her thigh with her out-of-character, last-minute English manicure. Chip prefers her half-eaten nails, even when they have raccoon poop under them.

Dammit, where is he?

She needs Chip to seal the deal. Needs . . . shakes her head in embarrassment . . . his money. The spider monkeys chatter behind her, mocking her, not sharing their secrets. In the distance, a lion roars a mouthful of lazy disappointment. Minutes crawl past—fifteen of them.

She remembers the day he wins the lottery. He's breathless, ecstatic, a happy mess of emotion. She recalls his stutters over the phone, his inability to look at her while he recounts his soon-to-be-famous tale of how he actually hands his ticket to his bro a few hours before the numbers are processed, and then takes it back an hour later when Bro says he doesn't believe in lotteries.

When he sees her in person that night, there is no kiss hello, no jabs about her animal day. He simply recounts and recounts his same story to her, each time embellishing his words a little more and frequently interjecting with the periodic, quickly-becoming-stale phrase *I can't believe it!*

Then he promptly poops his pants. Right in Perfect Pizza. He ignores the stench and keeps talking, while CoCo gets a very clear idea of how he'll be much later in the care of a Moonscape Home of his children's choice. When Chip and CoCo finally rise up from their chairs and stumble out, she follows him, sees the dark stain on the butt of his pants and avoids stepping in little dark drips that splash out the bottom of his tired pantlegs.

Back at the zoo, in *there and now*, CoCo endures another twenty agonizing measures of time then sighs, defeat creeping in. With an obligatory nod, Pinstripe lopes away with his suited dignitaries and leaves her standing there staring at the opening ribbon on the ground, muddy and forgotten. She closes her heart and walks away.

BUBBLE SANDWICH

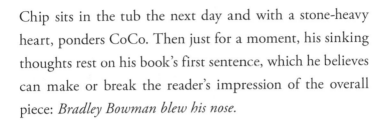

Chip sits in the tub the next day and with a stone-heavy heart, ponders CoCo. Then just for a moment, his sinking thoughts rest on his book's first sentence, which he believes can make or break the reader's impression of the overall piece: *Bradley Bowman blew his nose.*

It starts just like that. Then just as the medium-sized bubbles pop in his hand, CoCo is gone. He hears her voice, mostly the taunting one that teases him and gives him serious heck. She arches an eyebrow whenever he messes up. When she questions what he's saying, she traces his earlobe with the edge of her smooth pinkie finger while he pauses, shallow in his own thoughts.

What would you do with a million dollars?

Spend it!

On the computer side of his mind, he plays a nonstop disc of what he'll do with the money: give to charity, many of them, and right away to show what an obedient citizen he is; wander lots with CoCo, wherever she wants to go; invest in stix and binz, er, get advice first on what to invest in; collect new cars, as many as he likes, most of them missing tops; buy old refurbished mansions, a few in each area he frequently travels to; oh yeah, get the old folks set up in the best Moonscape home money can't buy; maybe throw Bro some dough; and of course, help CoCo with her animal dream. There, that should do it.

Thank God, it's the '50s, and I'm not taxed on it, he muses, unable and unwilling to just forget about the money. He's focused enough to realize the Win guys killing him share a giant deal, including access to his identity and, therefore, his winnings. Plus, further access to his resulting investments, such as PalmTech, Total Weather Control, and the Boobies Shop account—providing the coffee giants with enough drugs to addict people for life *and* drive them crazy.

He drives himself nearly insane by rerunning and rerunning his "spend list" over and over in his mind—well, in half his mind.

Refurbished mansions, maybe five, one in each area . . .

On his best writing days, he thinks up wildly passionate stuff for CoCo: *I need to gently suck the tendon in your neck and wrap my lips around your exposed wrist . . . The warmth of your breasts makes me shiver, electricity pulsing through my veins . . . I want to pull you down in the wet grass, peel off*

*your drenched pants and make love, the water streaming down
your thighs . . .*

Off one hand, he wipes the bubbles with an equally bubbly
hand, causing hundreds of them to burst spontaneously,
giving off that foamy, multi-popping sound. He doesn't
press his palms together to make an airy sandwich,
marveling at bubble physics. Instead, he taps his toby-tall
to his palm and speed-dials her, knowing she'll feel each
ringtone vibrate along her own palm. It rings and rings,
each shrill mocking him, unwilling to offer him that oh-
so-familiar *hello* she breathes, excited and busy but always
there for him at the top of her heart.

As his own heart slows on the cold stairs, his visions clear,
and he reruns entire conversations, past scenes, everything
leading him up to this point, his life not flashing before
him but rather meandering around itself, creeping along,
reminding him of who he was, who he had become. Who
he is now—a bloody heap of pagan flesh.

"Do ya think we should get married . . . or sumthin?" he
asks her one day over English onion soup.

"Nah," she teases. "Very old-fashioned. And way too
dangerous."

"You do work with wild animals every day," he notes, a
girlish grin playing his face.

"Much safer," she delivers smoothly. "At least I can leave the cage whenever I like."

"What about kids?"

"What about 'em?"

"Would you like to have some?" He blushes.

"Someday, you know, in the future?"

She pushes him down in the wiry grass. "Then I'd *never* get to leave my cage!"

Losing her ices his heart, makes him feel like he's preserved in a snowy grave, coolly protected, kept alive only by the memory of her warmth. As he thinks of her, his pool of blood cools and thickens around him, shielding him from his own life.

"Hey, mate, whare ya off to next?" Robere's voice cuts in as Chip is dragged toward a deafening light. Robere looks him up and down, doing that raised eyebrow move. The man's shoulders look strong and comforting, like warm, gentle rocks he could wrap himself around if he chooses to. As a senior, he'll be the cat's purr.

"Ay, nowheres special," Chip replies casually, picking up the talk only they share.

"C'mon, ya takin' that wee girl o yers, arn't ya now?" He gives him a wink and a nod of his pale yellow waves, eyes blue and menacing as the ocean on a crisp day.

"Not this time, lad." Chip sighs, searching for a way out as he feels his cool shield slipping away.

"Well, how's about some beers then?" he tosses back in time-worn macho-bond talk, knowing when to back off. "We'll celebrate." He flips his hair out of eyes and shrugs, one hand in the back pocket of his overused spray-on denim. They end up at a bar called Big Bruce.

FIRE-HYDRANT PEE SPREE

SUMMER 2050

CoCo turns her face to the dying cub and sighs. She needs a distraction from the dying Chip in the next room, not a reminder.

"Losing two animals," she breathes, blaming herself. She walks away from raspy breathing and peers out the window. *How to prevent this . . .* She limps back to the table and counts the spots on the little belly that rises and falls as if air is being pumped into it by some unknown force.

Back at the window, she can see the elephant compound and all the spectators surrounded in awe of Jumbo's five-minute, fire-hydrant pee spree. This time nobody gets splashed.

CoCo loves her work and is openly passionate about it. From the time she's six, she knows animals, the way they think, how they'd like to control the world. Although she can't collect every delicate specimen she finds (she lives in a tiny apartment with her dad), she follows through in her imagination.

The tumor-infested mouse she rescues from bullies lives in her sock drawer, while the battle-scarred tabby sleeps while wrapping the length of itself around the base of the toilet bowl.

Her dad is understanding of her needs, and so he digs up an ancient set of encyclopedias much beyond her comprehension—all part of his easygoing way to encourage self-teaching.

CoCo's quest for animal knowledge never slows, and after college, she finds herself tripping off to zoos all over the place, first as an apprentice with expanding connections. Her dream is to one day operate her own zoo, preferably near her home city so she can keep an ear on a raccoon family she's been feeding on her back porch.

"Now that we've got money, babe, you can have your zoo and eat it too!" pipes Chip as their hands clasp after a session of wild monkey chasing.

Giggling, she rolls to face him better, creating cleavage where there would normally be none. He squints in involuntary disgust as an image of Mom flashes, she in her yellow polka-dot dress stooping over to kiss him good night.

What would you do with a billion dollars?

I'd start a business with my mom.

As a boy, he notices all the neighbors let theirs hang out; he's surrounded and feels weakly compelled to ignore the blobs hanging in his face every time he plants his butt reluctantly in the hairdresser's shampoo chair and has to peer up the soap-aroma armpits of a coiffed girl or stroll past a lady bent over doing serious gardening, her sunburned breast flesh wobbling, moist with sweat and dabbled with irregular splotches of caramel color.

FLIPPIN' BLUE HAIR

Sweat streaks Chip's mud-caked face as he lies belly up in the cot next to CoCo's animal compound. He tries to force his eyes shut, but they feel glued open. He smells CoCo, senses her heavy exhaustion.

"Talk to me." She melts in that perfect radio voice. He remembers her on top of him, massaging away his knots.

"Co . . .," he trails off, frustrated by his lack of available words.

"Damn lottery," she sighs. "I still don't give a rat's boobs about the crap money."

He loves her direct approach. She's a good person. He knows it in his heart and wants to marry her for that reason only. She laughs whenever he brings it up.

Staring fully at the ceiling, he tries to focus. Lottery . . . Lucky numbers . . . CoCo . . . Lucky number 7.

Ah, be careful what you wish for, the psychic lady hisses, flipping her blue hair out of her crinkled eyes. Bluebox blue it is. He'll never forget that pasty face, her wicked smile. It's CoCo who drags him there.

The second Chip sees the blue-haired lady, he knows two things for sure: She's for real, and he's a believer. She has two simple messages through the hazy, heavy, taunting details: He will come across a great sum of money (*hah!*) and end up using it to change the world (*double hah!*).

He tries hard to concentrate on CoCo's words as she describes in rapid detail how she used her telepathy skills to rescue him as he was giving up, bloody and dying.

"When you were found and your parents contacted, they didn't want to save you and break the Suicide Prevention Law. I tried to tell them this was your second life, that there was no way you'd cut it short after winning the lottery, that some corrupt people must have Tasered you and left you like that . . . so I shipped you here . . . You've always loved Africa . . . I'm trying to save a lion cub too . . . We'll see which one makes it . . .," she trails off.

As he sinks back down through his bloody consciousness, Chip spots the twenty on the ground before Bro does. In one motion, the bigger boy stoops and scoops.

"Hey!" protests the smaller boy with the big ears.

"Sorry, Bro, I don't share my money."

The two of them find their way home, time lost in jabs and jokes, squinting in the lowering sun, baseball bats propped against dusty shoulders. Later, when everyone's asleep, Chip slips the twenty in Bro's piggy bank and shrugs in the gift of enclosing darkness.

RICH LIES

Chip spirals through deep black, trying to reach CoCo, trying to get back to her, *talk* to her. Then a phrase comes to him.

To be or not to be . . . rich.

Before he wins, it's as black and white to him as hot coals and cold potato salad. From Dad, he hears stories about mysterious lottery winners who squirrel away their winnings under mattresses and somehow just fade away; he won't be that type. If he ever wins. He's just tired of bills, always worried about the money, never able to buy the things he needs, like Italian ice cream and his own Moon bus. Both at once would be nice.

He's cursed with wavy red hair. With money, he could be straight all the time. He could buy CoCo things, if he could ever figure out what she wants. They could hand-glide into the breeze forever and never come back, not until they're old and happy. And yes, with a pet or three.

To look at him when currency exists, you'd never know he's one to obsess over the mighty loonie. His wild red waves and casual slump remind many of someone fresh out of tech school. Big brains and bigger ideas. The idealist part, they have accurately pinned. He thinks he has time to make money *and* keep his girlfriend.

But to his own demise, he can't stand the thought of wasted money, especially the government's loot.

"Supposed superbugs have proven to be extremely expensive," he writes in his secret *Secret Superbugz* book. *"SARS sliced nearly $140 billion out of the world economy in the early 2000s, and by the end of the decade, it was discovered the government spent a whopping amount on swine flu vaccines based on old information."*

He shudders at the thought of yet another Ebola blast. But he doesn't think of the sick and dying people. He mourns for the millions of government monies spent on trying to save those who are already gone, wasting efforts and funds on a lost cause—something he would never do, even as an inexperienced and disadvantaged youth.

Even at twenty, he has the brains of a hyper-focused genius and the bones of a dinosaur. He's heavy; he sleepwalks, pulls himself through the days, tosses against the nights, lives the life of an average bro, desperately prays—well, maybe not praying—for a change to put an end to his misery. (Given his current life or death state, that old *careful what you wish for* adage comes to mind.) He dreams of reincarnating himself as something grand, someone . . . unforgettable.

He tries suicide once or twice but grows so bored with the concept he gives up. There must be a better way to die. He can't leave via simply being killed; that's just embarrassing, been overdone. Everyone else glorifies killing oneself to the point of tedium. He needs a brand new idea.

There it is, just up ahead. The perfect parking space. Shady, spacious, roomy for his *mobile*, made for him. A man wearing a scraggy mustache in a Smush car floats in ahead of him. Steals his spot. Trying to be oblivious to the anger catching in his throat, Chip stares straight ahead as if he doesn't even see the dude, begins to whistle, and coasts off to find a better spot. Not that it really matters. It's just the everyday work parking lot with tons of slots, not exactly a Worms game or anything worth getting upset over.

He hears the knock again and slams his head under his pillow.

"Not now, Mom!" he whines, on the verge of final exasperation. The door creaks open, and there she is, her gorgeous gray hair hanging in a neat bob, framing a face that's gentle and oblivious. Now at the foot of his bed, she raises an eyebrow at him and places her hands on her hips the way strict moms do. She's wearing a plain navy shirtdress with a banana-candy colored thong underneath. He knows she's wearing a thong because when he's five, he sees a drawer full of them in her room. He already knows her second life will be full of hilarious sex and rocking adventure.

"You promised," she encourages, never turning her head, not even when the garbage ship floats past, waking all the neighbors. He sighs a heavy fake sigh and manages to pull himself up to rest on his wide palms. But he forgets to tree out last night, and that sets off his jTunes, and they get a blast of *Sugar Sex* fully plugged.

"Sorry," he mumbles with one quick brush of his thumb to silence the noise radiating from his hand.

"You really should do more around here. It's just not fair," she says sweetly before turning and walking silently out, the corners of her mouth turned down. He watches her aging form shuffling away and envies her, *can't wait* to grow old. He's only forty.

"You know the smell of garbage makes me chuck," he complains to himself as he flops back into the pillows Uncle Noron stitched up for him.

Chip's dying state stays its attention on Mom, how she lives and dies. With great clarity, he sees into her inner world, understands everything as he nears his own version of God.

NAKED AND BRUISED

In Chip's mind, Mom is a gal, plain and simple; just wants to get married and have a garden. Like in the ancient 1950s. From her flat denim sneakers to her small crinkled eyes, it never dawns on her to have any other expectations. Digging, digging, always digging in the dirt, trying to find something not there.

Maybe, just maybe, behind this jagged rock will be the answer . . .

Inside each of her flowers is a colorful promise that life is swell and good. She beams at the yellow roses; the color is off-limits for her clothes. The red peonies wink from their bed of dry dirt; they know she's drawn to their deep taunting fire.

Strange, she ponders one day while on her knees, clawing around the new fern, trying to get it more air. (She's careful not to set off any palm sensors in her hands as she presses them gingerly across the dirt.) Yes, strange how her husband bans her from wearing any bright colors yet seems to like it on the skeletal bikini images stealing space on his palm calendar. She thinks of them now with their tiny fake boobs and copycat buzzed silver hair. She'd like to touch one of them, even if they aren't real. Suicide Suzies they're called, dolled up on their last days so people can remember them as they weren't.

One thing Mom does believe in is anti-Christmas. To celebrate, she, of course, does the traditional thing—plants some sort of pine somewhere in her town, in true hopes of someday replacing all Christmas trees ever harvested—but she makes sure to do right by herself, to her very core, just like they outline in the Ex-Mass brochure.

Like with RRR recycling at the turn of the century, it's taking time for people to catch on to the DDD law. Do It, Donate, and Plant Delilas. For Mom, that means meticulously packing up a small truckload of stuff—a little of it valuable, most not—bugging Dad to hover it away to the Salvation Army. Since all commercial stores now close for the month of December, she has her pantry well stocked with goods, especially canned water and red rice. Prepared for the best, she always is.

So when the first wave of do-gooders come to town, she's ready to bring back the old-time notion of helping neighbors and smiling to strangers, complete strangers. She's all for it. The movement begins quietly at the onslaught of 2012, as a grassroots Get-Back-to-Happiness campaign, and picks up slow momentum over the next twenty years with people scrambling to join in, leaving work early to visit people in young folk homes, refusing to race other cars to red lights, and donating everything from blood to sexual favors.

Mom likes how the massive slow-driver fines are finally demolished. (She's collected twenty-seven tickets to be exact and owes the government thousands.) But she's not thinking about that and how if she doesn't pay the money soon, she'll go to jail. (She'll just get her wealthy son to bail her out.)

What she's mostly thinking about these days is the new Open Copulation Act. Apparently, *they* claim infrequent sex leads to violence and greed, so new Sex-on-the-Spot clinics open, and the government pays for people to get some relief in a safe, humane manner. (Now government-induced, permanent birth control, that's another thing. More on that later, much later, along with the Parent Licensing Program, PLP for short.) Yes, disease plays its part in Sex-on-the-Spot, but with suicide becoming so popular, many really don't care.

Mom guesses clinic sex is far better than doing it all over the place in public, as is becoming the norm. She will never admit that sometimes the height of her day involves taking a greedy stroll through the park, sitting on a park bench, and watching people go about their business in various positions and scenarios.

One day she nearly gets involved in such a scene. A woman waddles toward her, ugly breasts heaving and thighs pink from frolicking in the grass. Mom decides she loves the mole on her left, lower cheek, can't stop staring at it, finds herself rising and lowering, her breathing coming from deep behind her ribcage.

Should she sit, or should she go?

In the not-too-far distance, the woman's friend sighs and runs his thumbs through his shaggy beard, trying to loosen crumbs from his quickie Cheetos fetish. Just as Mom is about to moan out, her sight set on the sinking sun, the huge square of fire it is, Dad shows up with a stern pout and, once again, drags her away, naked and bruised.

Caught ya blue-handed, woman!

As she's floated home, she thinks of blood and remembers the days when blood banks are so overstocked they have to kick everyone out of town hall permanently so they can build emergency storage units. That's before they have to add on to those buildings to make more room for the millions of body bags needed to keep up with the suicides.

Two years later, folks remember it as the Year of Rules because along with Ex-Mass comes another smashing anti-money law that requires every citizen to log their good deeds, and by month's end, if it doesn't add up, harsh punishments are handed out. Mom has a super good friend who ends up in jail simply because she forgets to record all the times she helps relatives in their gardens.

"That Penny sure deserves to get to heaven." Mom smiles, wondering if she's made it there.

Dad, as he drags Mom along, is a boy's man. Always has direction, purpose, and is stern enough about it. Lives by the old code that overrates youth and its bulging insecurities. To hell with the new glorification of old age and its so-called visionary perks, its obsession with controlled reincarnation. He will live one life and live it right the first time. And without animals. Dammit!

One day at the mall, Mom eyes a flowing red dress plastered with huge vibrant blue and yellow flowers.

"You'll look like a *clown* in those colors," he snorts. He walks one aisle away from her special dress and plucks a tight gray number with a neckline plunging to the breastbone. "You'll be *beautiful* in this." He smiles, not noticing the clouds in her eyes.

CRY OF A WATERFALL

Floating, floating in a time so close to death, so near he can smell its frosty burn, Chip turns to the girl on the bed and tosses her tight candy-pink dress. It lands on her head, concealing a smirk and last night's smudged eye shadow.

He recalls the day before at LottoSex Park, just doing it in public, as is the norm. He's splayed on an old wooden park bench, and she's on top of him, grinding away without expression, as if he's simply another dirty spot on the floor she's trying to scrub out because her death depends on it.

They aren't completely naked, and passersby mostly ignore them. But even though it's completely okay to have sex, open sex, on a park bench these days—gawed, it *is* 2050—it doesn't feel right to him. He's shy and wishes he has his CoCo to get naked with. Just her. Even in this time of *friends*.

"You always smell like other women," she complains the other day. His own sense of smell is virtually invisible. Working with animals teaches her to be aware of a yellow jacket about to give birth or the cry of a waterfall.

Wait! Is that CoCo's voice calling in to him? Oh god, she's saying something . . . What is it? What was it?!

Something about money. Chip suffers a conventional, typical relationship with money that still strangles most of the population.

He remembers a woman winning a big one in 2014. Four jobs Abbey Workalot has to quit. Everyone is jubilant for her, mesmerized as if she's just accomplished an amazing feat that requires talent and deserves recognition. But then she disappears, the news guessing she's changed locales and names . . . just because she can. What the public doesn't see is the fancy manicure her hand wears as it sinks, along with her other naked body parts, to the bottom of Lake Losers.

You can't drag it with you.

Chip examines banks with a cynical eye and sighs every time he slips past their sneaky, sliding doors, mistrusting every float screen, staring in awe every time he sees a big safe in the back.

How to get in there . . .

He plays lottery constantly, dreaming of winning it big, all along knowing it's more of a silly, unobtainable sidetrack.

He invests in toys when he can. A motorcycle, hot tub, second car, extra house to rent out to folks on the wrong side of the trails. Although it's illegal and he hasn't yet been caught, he rarely gives to charity, believing most of them study how to be fake panhandlers in some sort of back-alley school. He's cheap with his girlfriend, and although he loves her to bits, the real thought of marriage makes him shiver. Uncontrollably.

Why should he share everything?

In the middle of Chip's death dreams, a teacher peers at him over the tops of her spectacles and sighs.

"And, young man, just what do you want to be when you grow up?"

"I wanna be rich."

She sighs, turns away for a few seconds, just long enough to check the time strapped efficiently to her wrist and roll her eyes toward the dusty ceiling. Only fifteen minutes to the next coffee. She turns back to him, a faint smirk tugging her quivering mouth corners up when they really want to go down.

"And why do you want to become rich, Mr. Chip Munk?" she asks, hoping she sounds innocent and curious rather than cynical and probing.

"With money, I can change the world!"

HANDSOME BY MOM'S STANDARDS

Chip grows up dirt poor, on a sideroad on the edge of a small town named Duckdork. Just a concession away, Lake Scummud shimmers under the scorching sunset of a putrid summer night. Red-winged blackbirds squawk through the pines, and turkey vultures swoop overhead looking for roadkill. Folks adopt children instead of roads and keep their noses in other people's business as much as possible. (Complaints rise up from Henley next door when Mom puts up new sun-blocking blinds.)

The corner store still sells penny candy, although prices have risen to a quarter for two of those hard square pink bubble gums wrapped in unfunny comics. They eat meat, play outside in their yards, have beer-infested BBQs, and take to sledding in the snow months, when they wear real winter boots and ramble down snow-packed roads in pickups streaked with last fall's mud. Just another plain-faced, invisible corner of the world.

Chip's parents are typical, his life is what's expected of a boy born in 1985. A generation into anything fun, competitive, and later, electronic. And Chip is handsome by Mom's standards. So he grows up in a nondescript way, eats pizza on Friday nights, and excels in math. He's so poor they only order in pizza once a week and own only one game of Pretendo.

He hates his life, moves to the nearest city when he's old enough and becomes a quiet working stiff, just droning on and on like a reluctant working bee. He has a passive, some would say rather boring, personality, but nature stirs him.

The swoop of an eagle catching a field mouse is, in his eyes, pure joy. The smell of the hunt, survival, his toughest man instincts. He needs to keep in touch with his "female" side but finds it a difficult task. It's just easier to coast, live, and not feel so much.

Chip's dying memories are icy clear now. He finds the wee mouse behind his school, scoops it into an empty coffee cup, and hides it inside his jacket, safe from the wind.

"Hey, whatcha got?" demands a Billy. (Much later, such behavior would have barred him to a Mars clinic.) Chip turns and starts to walk briskly, but the Billy stops him. "Is it alive?" he probes, more annoyed than curious.

"Sorta," Chip mumbles. "He hurt his leg, and I was just . . ."

"Putting him in his misery?"

Chip nods, too afraid to move, the mouse squirming as if understanding.

"Let's see you do it!" The boy laughs. "Kill it!"

Chip stands frozen to the ground, his mind circling.

"Give it to me. *I'll* do it!"

They push and shove at each other, feet spread wide, bodies joined at the shoulders, faces red, the mouse peeking out with bulging eyes. Then the red ringlets appear, causing all of them to step back.

"Dammit, stop this idiotic behavior!" she demands with all the authority of a grown-up.

With a crazy look and one hand on her hip, CoCo holds out the other hand, forming a cup shape with fingers pressed together tightly, eyes never leaving Chip. Hands shaking, he hands over the tiny creature and is pulsed, somewhere in his brain, to her inner core, somewhere safe.

Two months after winning the lottery, Billy shows up at his back door.

"Hey, congrats," mumbles the now slicked-back-hair dude, a hint of wary sorrow on his brow. "You remember me, don't you? Trent." Obviously from the old-school-name generation. "I'd like to make things right by finally apologizing for my former barbaric self."

"Oh, I remember," says Chip, trying not to look defiant as he gently closes the door. And with that, he walks away, never to cross paths with this soul until nearly Nirvana time.

Chip is handsome by Mom's standards, broody and unapproachable by opinion of neighborhood boys. Fascinated with sex since his fourteenth birthday. Hot, steamy, naked, gushing sex. Would probably be addicted if he wasn't so shy. Spends much time in his room, not masturbating but dreaming of sex. Sex with women. Sex with men. Sex with all of them. In all variations. Not that he'll try most of his daydreams, but it's brain-pumping to think about.

CoCo lives too much in her head to bother with his obsessions. That's okay with him. He's only connected spiritually to her, the only one.

MONKEY LOVE

Aware he's running out of time in his current life, Chip flies from year to year, scene to life scene, all in his stiffening, restful state, his body aching to get out of its own skin.

In most of his visions, he sees CoCo. Short, dark, and the most interesting creature he's ever laid ears on. CoCo. Her tongue rapid fire, her eyes troubled beyond belief, her sense of fashion fun beyond ridiculous. But she takes chances, soars, and isn't afraid of anything besides insults. It's she who introduces him to *adventure* in the outdoors, and thus, their camping trips are born.

He wakes inside the tent in the end of night and sees her shadow against the tarp wall, a fuzzy blob next to the firelight just outside. Blob bends to stroke fire, blob straightens up, turns face toward tent door; he catches the outline of her face, the upturn of her nose, petite lips, then back to blob as she turns back and talks to the fire, movements stiff but unplanned.

He groans, rolls out of his sleeping bag, and yanks on the zipper . . . *ziiipppp* . . . so loud and foreign in a night that hears only distant animal shuffles. Blob shadow turns her head sharply in his direction.

"Hey!" she whispers hoarsely because she hasn't spoken in a while. She turns her head back to her fire and laughs. She laughs at him a lot. Not to ridicule him but because he's so ridiculous.

They meet while traveling. Both doing their jobs, he researching tech know-how for terrarium temperature gauges and she delivering boas to their proper habitat. She has a huge she-snake slung low across her shoulders when he sees her the first time. There he is, notepad in hand, scribbling down numbers. She wears red. That's all he remembers, that, her smile and that snake!

From her squinted eyes that day latches a radiance he can't quite grasp, let alone match. She takes him aside and becomes his mentor. Adventure, confidence, the one imprinted on his heart, literally. Some silly tattoo she talks him into. He's all nerves that day, she's brimming with dares, her best one yet. For him, anything for him.

She offers him her pet monkey, but he's not sure what to do with it. As he lies in the shade of an ancient apple tree, he strokes its coarse fur and wonders how to react to its ever-so-changing lips and quirky movements. He wants to love it so badly, but he just can't get past the darkness of it, the airy sounds that escape from it, the squeals it produces.

"Be a man," she challenges. "Just feed it what it wants."

"Romance is overrated," he tells her in the beginning. After two months, I-love-yous pour out of him. Everywhere he goes, he imagines her there. She's the center of his beautiful dream, the girl with short dirty fingernails and a tough fireworks spirit to match.

She always thinks him a bit of a nerd, and that makes her love him more. Not nerdy in appearance (her imagination often drifts over his broad forehead, down his strong back, and into his white boxers—always white boxers) but adrift somehow in his thinking. He's always elsewhere, wherever that is, dreaming, drifting, never demanding, never aware.

But when the money comes, he grows restless, careless, and mean. His words are quick and hurtful, his eyes dark, as if he hasn't slept in decades. Hidden angst erupts, changing him. On better days, he describes himself as more brazen, *living life to the fullest*, as cliché lottery ads brag.

One day they're shopping at a high-end men's clothing store where he labors over which suits to choose. She sits and sits and sits, while he floats into crisp shirts and allows flowing suit fabrics to caress him. Finally, she gets thirsty and mentions that maybe, just perhaps, it's time to go.

Yes, it's nearly time to go, time to die . . . Where is that bright light?

In a huff, he grabs everything in the change room, marches up to the till, and plunks it all on the ancient wood-grained polished countertop.

"I'll take *all of it*," he announces to the float monitor as if he'd just cashed in at old-time bingo. A man approaches behind them, and CoCo sees he has a single rose-colored shirt draped across his arm like an unaffected waiter in a fancy eatery. In his haste grabbing out his bulging wallet, Chip spills a roll of paper money on the floor, and the man behind stoops to help retrieve it.

"Just keep it, dammit! I don't have time for this," Chip hisses, his face red and angry.

Sheepishly, the man presses the roll of money into Chip's palm and shrugs.

"No, thanks," he mumbles politely. "We can't use paper bills anymore."

Chip is furious by now as he stuffs the useless paper deep into his pants pockets. He throws down the garments and leaves, CoCo dragging her feet behind. The polite man bares his wrist for the scanner.

Soon after, on another ugly summer day, the two of them run into a shop to escape the heat.

"I miss the good old days when your damn skin didn't nearly peel off from the damn sun." She smirks.

"But when we were young and hopeless," he reminds her, "the weather was starting to go crazy already. I was only twenty-nine when the first wind tunnel hit."

Tornadoes and wind tunnels, once obscure events observed in the news and met with slow shakes of the head to express detached pity, are now common day. Neighborhoods and buildings in constant repair from such natural disasters. Lives lost gaining in numbers. Just something else to dodge. Better to take your own life so you could use your dying thoughts to control your second time around.

Lying limply in his death cot, Chip takes CoCo's comforting hand and wishes it will rain. So this is what it's like in the end, wanting only favorite people around you as you slip away, every other concern in life fading slowly from the memory like events to be recalled from a long continuous dream.

Except for the thought of rain. He knows in his gut it will make the Earth feel good, maybe even grow some green. (At this point, everyone is cremated because of green space shortage.) Since he's soon to become part of the Earth, he figures water nourishment is a good thing. He's never squashed any spiders to move things along, but he loves a rainy day, the overcast light, the water-soaked bark of trees, some of it peeled back to reveal raw, gentle energy. The earthiness takes him in a breath as simultaneously close to life *and* death as he will ever get.

What he doesn't miss about the rain is recent water destruction . . . local washouts every month, an earthquake every Ex-Mass . . . weather gone a little haywire in 2020 now everywhere commonplace.

Their attention shifts to a rack of jeans in every unimaginable neutral color.

"God, I'm so sick of denim," she says. "Too cold in the winter, damn hot in the summer."

While he secretly wishes she'll invest in the new painted-on kind of jeans all the girls are wearing, bringing back memories of the oops-forgot-my-pants era of 2014 leggings, he nods in agreement.

"Well, when spring and fall used to happen, it was perfect," he replies with perfect timing, images of stickly legs and small flat butts in basic black boring leggings crossing his mind. Colorful leaves of years gone by float between their thoughts.

"Damn denim," she continues, fingering the hem of her patched Renaissance frock. "Way overrated if you ask me."

"I didn't." With a ballerina twirl and mouthy grin, he has chosen denims in hand, ready to give a go at them.

It's only then that the virtual salesclerk pipes, "This retro skinny butt version is sure to lure the robots."

He swipes his wrist across the tag's barcode, and an all-too-common beep confirms his treasure is paid for in full. Not waiting for the float screen to burp out a mechanized "thank you," they leave arm in arm, laughing, trying to dodge the scorching rays.

NO. 2 CUT

"You'll save yourself twenty grand if you nab it now," crazy Best Bud advises Chip shortly after his lottery win. Chip strokes his newly-clipped no. 2 cut and sighs. Behind Best, who also happens to be his financial advisor, is a row of original watercolor prints—the cheap imitation kind you find at every flea market—thinks Bud, although he knows they're one of the last authentic venues that still accept currency.

From somewhere really far away, CoCo brushes the hairs on his arm. The sun is brilliant, her hair soft, her legs smooth. "Hun! Buy me that ceramic doggie, please," she pretends to pout, the girly gig not part of her real character. He reaches in his front pants pocket, ignoring what is stirring there, and grabs a fistful of change, smacks it down, and turns to the woman of his life. It's like she's screaming, "Yes!"

Best grows impatient with Chip's increasing daydreams, every line creasing his already-stressed forehead.

"All right, all right," Chip mumbles, snapping back to the hair appointment. He nods a thanks to his HairBot (Human hairdressers are naturally replaced by robots because of the devastating effects of related chemicals.) With a dismissive wave of his manicured hand, Chip is off on his next money mission, and Best, with the rip-off watercolor print under his arm, is but a smudge in the wide scope of his day.

Best knows Chip is a clueless lottery winner, and he intends to make the most of it. When they meet over beers, Best can see the dollar gleam in his soon-to-be-companion's eye. He recognizes that look. He also knows, like any addict never intending to give up their vice, that they're helpless victims.

He later regrets getting in with the Win gang and helping them hunt down his best friend.

TIGER FACE

Chip's death dreams start to repeat themselves as he slips toward the light at the end of the bridge.

He turns to the robot girl on the bed and tosses her red dress. It lands on her head, concealing a smirk and last night's smudged eye shadow.

He turns his face away as she mechanically dresses and hobbles forward just enough to remind him she's not real. He stares himself in the mirror and at first comes up blank. Then he sees only the nose of a tiger sniffing back at him.

But there, *wait a minute*, he spots CoCo in the background of his irises, swooning and arching her back, doing one of her seductive swan dances. Naked, always naked. Steadying his arm under her back, he bends to kiss her pale neck, strokes her forearm until the baby hairs stand up straight, and holds her to him.

"I'll never let you fall." He laughs as he holds her like that, and she lets herself sink into him, like a tired body on moon foam. "And I'll never let you go," he breathes.

WHITE CURLS

A boom hits Mom square in the chest, striking the life out of her—baby crying, adolescent girl with knobby knees, teen partygoer, white wedding, son born, travels with Dad—all flashes within seconds and then gone, a waste that never was. Her white curls flutter in the breeze as the pirates jump the yacht named Gilligan. Dad, in his skipper hat and scruff, is frozen on deck, a small tear running its course.

Then he's gone, no space for flashbacks, his only thought on getting to heaven, whatever that is.

At the same second, a car cracks another one broadside as Chip watches from behind, his heart stopping for a second. All is a blur and a blow to his senses. Flashing lights, blood on the road, an officer urging him to leave his car. He doesn't know the victims, all of them dead and hanging out of their still-hovering vehicles, but it hits him like a killer sneaking up on his prey, poising his shovel, ready to strike.

Standing on the side of the road, watching them clean up the bloody mess, his thoughts stream to his parents.

The first and only cruise of her life and Mom doesn't even want to go.

"Who will take care of the gardens?" she inquires, a real tone of sadness and worry in her small cracked voice. Chip puts an apricot-scrubbed palm on her bony shoulder and sighs as if he's the parent about to teach one of life's long lessons.

"Mom, listen . . . you've never gone anywhere."

"I don't *need* to go anywhere."

She stares him blank in the face. "I'm happy right here. You know, traveling is very much . . . overrated," she adds smugly, proud of her big word. "You've got all the preparation beforehand, the changing of the palm money, leaving everything back home in good hands, then there's a new language to grasp, strangers everywhere . . . we don't even know a lot about sailing. Besides, we're old."

She winks when she says the word "old." For two reasons. One, she's from the old school when folks actually dread growing old. Two, she knows her son is from the new school where growing old is a treasure.

"That's why I'm giving you lessons. Take as long as you want. It's all set up with the yacht club. Ginger and MaryAnn are the best teachers there, both plan to die on a boat. Try it out for the summer, and if you don't feel 100 percent ready, well then, go the next summer, only when you're totally ready. It'll be the trip of a lifetime. I promise."

"Well . . . " She stalls, words failing her. She blinks her blue eyes, thinking. "Let's just book a Mars quickie. That'll do." She grins, proud of getting herself out of a nervous situation.

Chip shakes his head, grinning back.

"You know that's a one-way trip to nowhere."

Ever since the first successful Mars trip in 2025, everyone and their sister wants to go. First, it's a big deal, colonizing the place with the first fifty people, experts even advising the first batch be female, already inseminated when they leave. Tough ones they want, those who can handle getting red dust under their fingernails all day short. After a while, just like any other traveling trend, it becomes commonplace with folks coming and going, palming their money away, much like the Florida craze of yester-month.

People now take the Moon bus, stopping by to eyeball the craters, much to the dismay of those promoting the struggling Rockies. The entire earthly traveling thing has finally hit a wall as most favor out-of-planet experiences, which are now mandatory on most resumes.

The modern man that he is, Chip doesn't steal into the hype, even with talk of Venus travels on the horizon.

Mom glances in Dad's direction, but he's busy trying to fold up a complicated map. He has a bunch of sailor gear spilled out on the table; he's more than ready to go.

"Your son's got a valid point," he says more sternly than intended. The hound dog saggies under his cheeks shake slightly with his next words. "It's time you and I lived it up awhile." After smacking down the map, all crumpled as it is, he folds his arms, and she knows he's going, with or without her. "I'm game," he announces, not moving a muscle.

"Now then," she replies as confidently as she can, her small dark eyes darting back and forth, "it'll be my first and last."

Chip meanders through the lives of his parents, drifts back and beyond to the doors of their childhoods. Just as those doors are about to fling open, he finds his thoughts at a hectic Hill Street Blues type of police station.

What would you do with a trillion dollars?

I'd sail south 'til the butter melts!

"The pirates were after their access codes," states the detective blandly, peering up over his specs at Chip as if to say "Ain't it obvious?"

Chip sits in the dog-leather chair and contemplates this. His right thumb poised, he considers making a call, then changes his mind, taps the brain screen away, and uses both sides of his brain to take this all in. He absently nudges his foot against the detective's desk and then his questions erupt.

"How did they . . . ?" he trails off. Since the Win people have sent him to public speaking school, his words sound a little foreign to him, detached, more like the beginning of a speech than a heartfelt question.

"You're rich. Therefore, your folks are—were—rich, and as you know, some people will do anything to get those codes."

"Have their codes been hacked yet?"

"Dunno. We're doing everything we can to get to them first. When we do, their estate will be rightfully handed over to you."

"The estate?! I don't care about the estate!" Chip explodes then immediately calms, recalling his Win training that readied him for the public nose. "I just want to know who the hell killed my parents."

The detective clears his throat, clearly making no apologies for what he's about to say.

"I'm afraid *you* did, sir." Now he looks truly apologetic. "You and your money."

Exactly two weeks after that meeting, Chip is called somewhere to identify Mom's hand, and as it sits in its box, all pale and toad-like, perfectly at home, number-crunchers already scrutinizing screens in their heads, working on handing Chip his rightful estate.

Exactly one week later, Chip has his hacker and, therefore, his estate. The guy's nickname is The Professor, and this leads, after much research, to Chip's first clue that the Win people are not as they appear. But unlike a slap on the tummy, the inkling comes to him like a small black cloud that quickly floats away to reveal the everlasting sunshine he's become so rightfully accustomed to.

But The Professor is not the murderer. No, that turns out to be Mr. Howel, a character launched into his own second life at the end of County Road 117, thanks in whole to a network of desperate people Chip uses along his way to richdom.

Chip donates the entire estate to BeerBellies Anonymous, a group aimed to help folks grow their bellies as huge as humanly possible without exploding. For entertainment, Chip has been tracking the group and following its expansion. After becoming famous, he nearly joins the group but then quickly realizes it will be a bad idea to explode and leave all his riches behind so soon. It is, however, part of his suicide research.

Shortly after he wins the lottery, Chip has his first serious talk with Dad.

"C'mon, *controlling the weather?* What kind of crock is that? Really?"

"It's my biggest investment, Dad. Everyone wants it. Tourism will go nuts, and we'll be rich!"

Dad raises one quizzical eyebrow and shakes his head in frustration, as if they've been over this and over that and why hasn't it sunk in?

"You always were the kookiest one of the bunch," he says with a low growl. "Money hungry since the day you were born. Heck, you'd even go without food if it meant more numbers on paper!"

"It's not just numbers, pops, it's my life," Chip announces as if he's just taken a stand back in 1999 and told Dad he's gay.

"Yes, son, it *is* your life. But it's *not* ours, and we want *no* part of it."

At some point later, Mom lines up her suitcases along the quilt-covered bed, stands back, and sighs.

"I wish he wouldn't make me go."

Bro chooses his words carefully as he's trying extra hard for some time away from his parents, whom he has lived with, in the same house, since he was born.

"We just want you to have fun. Git packin'!"

"Me and Chip will take care of the flowers." (A permanent watering ban means personal vegetation is fed water replacement pellets.)

She sighs, defeat setting in.

"Should I take my pink high heels, the ones I never wear?"

Bro's hazy thoughts float to the notion of high heels, trying to make sense of how people, mostly men now, insist on hobbling around on such painful stilts. Then he thinks of

Chip and how he wastes money on Mom by buying any color of shoes she demands—and any size.

"You could do some good, you know," he tries to reason one post-Win day with the wayward rich man. A few seconds pass.

"For a change," Bro dares to add, smirking and trying to be off-handedly casual with a remark only siblings can pull off.

"Some groups are not part of the big fraud. They're real, and they help people. Really."

What big fraud?

"I *am* doing good," Chip finally says. "I've donated to every God-knows-what group already." Chip wants so badly to add the word "stupid" in there somewhere, but of course, he doesn't.

As Chip hovers above his own death, he flashes to the worst Bro memory. It's behind the arena, a group of hockey guys taunting his slow brother in the lowering sun, their silhouettes stark on the chain-link fence, one bent at the waist in a menacing manner, finger poking at Bro who stands stiff, scared inside but being a man on the exterior.

"What a stupid idiot!" someone shouts, prompting the inevitable. Chip emerges ten minutes too late from the changeroom to witness the bloody afterphysics. He learns it's all over Bro wearing the wrong color of shoelaces.

Why couldn't he never get that right?

Chip wonders as he floats to heaven. Doesn't his brother understand what people expect? "Sheesh, Bro." He shudders. "Bright clothes finally got banned." He stares down at his own neutral-gray bodysuit and neutral-black shoes, silently craving hazard orange for this trip.

FURRY EYEBROWS

Along the way, just below the clouds, Chip again hears the familiar voice of his Best Bud.

"This invention will make us mills!" pipes Best, peering over his trendy, thick-framed specs that make you look at his furry eyebrows. Chip has a real urge to reach out and touch them, to see for real if they feel like the caterpillars of their youth. It also amazes him that Best still wears glasses. So retro of him, he snorts under his breath, thanking modern tech for his own eyeball replacements. Twenty-twenty vision has never been better . . . well, except for the few poor souls who can't afford a match and go eyeless for a while.

"Think of it! A series of numbers, letters, and symbols embedded in the human palm. Everything is recorded there and just scanned on demand. ID, banking, thinking, maybe even human transporting like in *Star Trek*! No more dirty money to fool with, and no more credit card fraud. We could be rich—"

"I already *am* rich," he reminds his new-old best friend, one of many who happen to pop back out of the walls at the precise moment he wins.

They used to catch bullfrogs in Mr. Kramer's pond, play NinPlendo, or just fool around in the long grass behind the only convenience store in town.

"Well, that's the point. With my inventive brains and your endless financial support, we could really rock this thing, take it to the top, help make . . . the future!"

Chip considers this for a moment, then nods mechanically, something he's done a lot of lately. Wherever the money wants to go, it goes, with or without him, he's decided, sinking lower into his armchair of miserableness.

All it takes is a shrug from Chip, partial access to his money, and PalmTech is born.

"The World Bank has announced today the end of currency as we don't know it," pipes the newsperson in that authoritative I-don't-really-care tone. "Now that everyone is *palmed*, money in its physical form"—dramatic pause—"is history."

CoCo leans forward in her Jeep and turns up the dial. Stubbornly old-fashioned, she refuses to get volume controls embedded behind her ears.

"Well, there's his first investment making tailway," she mumbles, wondering how to get rid of the small stash of fifties in her purse.

Then she's back in time, back in his arms, just two months after he wins the jackpot. That day she stomps out of bed and violently throws on her robe, tying the sash so tight it's squeezing her tummy like very-old-school jeans. He lies there yawning, unable to even open his eyes to her beauty. She senses something is off with his lovemaking, his apathetic response to her nakedness.

"Sorry, hun, I'm just so exhausted from all that paperwork with Win, all the meetings. I just want to make the right decisions, that's all."

She decides never to make love with him again.

"By the end of the year," the radio dude interrupts, droning in his self-important, deep voice, "*everyone* is to turn in their cash—that is *all* paper and coins—to their banks, and in turn, those sums will be trans-formatted into the PalmTech they've already been assigned."

"Aha, just where are the bad old days?" adds the announcer. Remember waaaaay back when the penny died?" But deep up, it's not the penny's death that has him worried.

ADDICTION OF
THE DECADE

Hovering just above the clouds now, Chip's body feeling weightless, his mind, not racing as he thinks might happen, but seeming to slow down like a thick mud, the name of a coffee shop sign stands out like a sore toe, just up ahead: Boobies—named after a cat groomer and appealing to nostalgia milked from such a long-gone profession. There's Boobies on the sign, the trademarked skinny black cat famous for lapping up his mugged coffee while smiling his drunk cat smile. One eye, tooth glistens, like a simple 1950s ad.

Chip shuffles his feet and joins the rest of the weary addicts seated at long communal tables equipped with hover order screens in front and selfie pouring paraphernalia. It's much like the old bars in the old days, before coffee became five times the hit of alcohol.

"Extra large thriple-thriple," he quips to the screen, then bares his right wrist to scan-pay, quickly adding, "Own mug." There, that saves him a buck!

"Sir, will you be driving within the next three hours?" flows the monotone woman voice, soft as an air-filled plastic bag.

Sighing, he changes his order to a medium thriple-thriple so he can get back to the skies sooner. He eyes the others as they fill their takeout cups with black sloshing java—the same cups penetrated with dickotine—a trace amount, just enough so that when the glue lining of the cups come into contact with water of a certain hot temperature (water laced with conformaminiti, judgeaholix, angrifel, bloatedbellaise, leechoderm, legrabamonee, and deblameit drained into it by the local Tetro plant before it even reaches victims' taps, thereby causing tickled tempers, lackluster lust, vulgar vulgarity, undue venting of unfounded emotions, and greed beyond belief—and when mixed with well-offishness, super greed beyond belief)—and *bingo!*—the addiction of the decade.

But something is different in the eyes of these addicts. Sure they get cranky when they don't get it, similar to alcoholism or smoking of prior decades. Sure they refuse free coffee from old Tom Mortons down the street, who already enjoyed his height years ago. At their worst, these new addicts are known to illegally set their sprinklers so their next-door neighbors get the gift of water through their kitchen windows. But they're getting immune to the drug. Chip can see that. *Time to up the ante and give 'em a taste of real glue*, he thinks as he sits and pretends to scan hovering headlines. Aha, another venue for his almighty Win dollas.

As he sits sipping his liquid gold, the steam floating up to greet his nostrils put him in insta-heaven, he stretches out his right hand and taps his palm twice with his toby tall. "That idea," he coos into his fingertips, not waiting for a voice response. One brush of his thumb across his pinky nail, thirty seconds of deep thought in the human side of his brain, and he makes an abrupt switch back to his computer brain, pulls up the blue screen in his head, and begins to ThinkSketch. Twenty minutes later, he swooshes the image to his Squinto, Ontario contact (he has to concentrate extra hard to complete the swoosh to overcome interference from his human brain . . . something about morals getting in the way). *Within six months, Boobies Bars locations across the country have a new secret ingredient.*

At first, the change is barely noticeable. Drinkers clear their throats a little more, cough in the night, periodically scratch their necks without even realizing it. But soon unsquelchable squabbles in long Boobies Bar lineups and erratic driving out of Boobies air lots become the norm, even from sipping size small, the only size legally consumable immediately prior to driving.

Chip sits back in his white leather recliner and observes these changes from his skyline condo. He just wants to make another buck; he doesn't really want to change people in any *significant* way. Oblivious to what's really happening, he just assumes the world must be going mad on its own.

Controlling a coffee empire, *that* is something, he tells himself, and much more exciting than just owning one. And at that second, he's delirious with his decision the previous year to turn down the Boobies franchise opportunity that presented itself just after he won.

He had squinted at the ad closely. *Everyone loves coffee. Everyone loves money. A marriage made in heaven.* He thinks of his friend Big Deal from high school. The dork is a billionaire just by owning a bunch of coffee shops. Chip could do that. But as the seconds pass, he develops an even bigger dream, and his greed grows thrice the Grinch size.

In the 2020s, just after a temporary coffee shortage scare, it had been proven that worldwide takeout coffee was injected with something—he couldn't remember just what it was—but people drank it anyway. Then shortly after his Win, a sharp stem in his mind begins to grow because, as shallow as he is, he is also, after all, brilliant.

As the richest man on Earth, he has the chance to buy all the Boobies in the world, every single pair. (They are only sold in twos.) But the idea is about as bland to him as eating puppy pate for every meal, every day for a month—all too predictable. In that idea, there is absolutely nothing to look *forward* to.

SWEET VOICE

On his slow trip to heaven, Chip tries to concentrate on his next life, on how it will be. But money memories continue to take up what little brain space he has left.

999 billion—*for simplicity's sake, let's just call it a cool . . . or better yet . . . a hot trillion. Too bad, it's not a gazillion.* His mind tosses around the idea of how much money it really is. Like the concept of death, of that version of you being gone forever and ever—at least until you're reincarnated as a new person in your second life—the notion that he is now entitled to endless cash is unfathomable. He still has to read the thick document the corp sent him over his old Blueberry. Couldn't they just palm it over to him?

The document? *"How to Claim, Collect, Protect, and Invest Your New Assets."* A third of it is devoted to ads for rich hunks of Greenland and worldwide coffee empires. Interesting since the global coffee supply is expected to run dry by 2070.

He'll never forget the day he claims the money. A little nervous, he palms the corp and inquires about how to go about . . . er, getting his fortune. A woman's sugary voice simply tells him to arrive at head office on Liars Street within a week with the ticket and no worries, no ID, and no need for a witness.

"Don't people usually claim their prize where they buy their winning ticket?" He's baffled by the response of the sweet-smelling lady.

"No need for that, sir," she breathes. "That way, we can get right down to business and get you on your way. Congratulations." She speaks the last word differently from the rest. It has a couldn't-care-less feel to it, plus a slight edge of danger, hopefully public sex. He shakes his head to pause the dream, but it remains.

When he shows up to claim his prize, the experience is surreal. He's taken into a room with bright white walls and only one perfectly matted print of a glamorous toothy bald man holding a fist full of old cash. *TAKE YOUR WINNINGS TO THE TOP!* it shouts in bold black-font cliche. Then he's shown a chair in front of King's desk, and from that increment in time, the rest of his life is history.

BRAIN OF A DINOSAUR

Chip has always known Bro has the heart of a lion and the brain of a dinosaur. Not mentally challenged, just . . . slow. That had always bothered Chip. When he was small, he hoped and prayed—well, maybe not prayed—his sibling would mature into a *real* brother, one he could really look up to and copy. Bro was wiser than his words and simply shook his head at his younger brother's ideas.

Some of Chip's things were fun, like the time they went skinny-dipping in a neighbor's green-slime pool (Mz. Lake had been away on one of her extended vacays and had forgotten all about her high-maintenance, rarely-used chemical bath), but some of the stuff was, well, just wrong. He knew it in his heart. It just wasn't right to slice that frog in half and watch it tremble and bleed. And it just wasn't right what he did to Betsy-Sue down at Uncle Ned's farm.

Then there was another time.

"Hey! Get away from my garbage cans!" hollers Weiss Arse.

"Sorry!" Bro calls out, getting red in the face. "I'm just looking for Taxi's ball. It was maybe tossed in here by accident."

But Bro knows it's no accident. Chip is always pulling mean pranks, and this is the latest: hiding the dog's favorite ball.

But Chip loves his dog, loves him with such passion that people don't matter. Taxi, he can train and do tricks with.

Yes, he is in control of his own Taxi.

Bro begs and begs his brother not to play Lotteries. "What if you win?" he moans.

"Isn't that the point?" Chip monotones, scratching his balls.

"But I want you to stay the same. I really do."

"Trust me, Bro, nothing *ever* stays the same."

WRITING ON THE CLOUDS

Drifting his way past Mars by now, Chip feels the full impact of his only true love—words. His passion goes beyond collective sighs from every second person you meet, those who say they have a story to divulge but they're hesitant to bust open their closet desire to write. No, Chip is a born writer, and if a single day passes without him putting his thoughts down, he feels anxious, nearly crazy with restlessness.

In his dying state, all this creative purpose balls itself up like a wad of newspaper in his human mind where it unfolds and spreads into an eternal book, his own personal story written on the clouds. He knows it's near the end. The beginning.

His keen ability to focus allows him the patience to methodically research numerous topics of interest. Especially involved with current events, he follows, records, and questions outbreaks affecting health of the masses. Out of that is born his *Superbugz* book, and through his obsession, he ends up with unique, insightful quips: *Funny how the virus name suddenly switched from swine flu to H1N1, rather clinical sounding with a hidden connection to pigs.*

When Chip returns from his post-Win vacay in the scorching sands of overrated hotspots of the world, a tall, dark, and ugly man shows up at his door back home.

"Hello, I'm Mr. BigWinns, colleague of Mr. Right, and I'm pleased to finally meet the man who's won the biggest lottery in history!"

"Hi," Chip monotones through the crack in the door. "Never let in strangers," Mom had warned in her old-fashioned ways. "They might try to steal your thoughts."

"May I come in?"

"Sorry, I'm busy right now." Chip shifts his weight to his other sock foot and sighs as if the man has just interrupted a million and two tasks.

BigWinns gently pushes on the door with his toby tall.

"I need to warn you about the scam that winners in your position usually fall prey to."

Silence and then . . .

"Scam?"

BigWinns clears his throat, strokes his 'stache and repeats his rehearsed lines until he has Chip on the couch staring into his eyes, moaning, scared, and scribbling his autograph on important papers.

Back in his den, King is pleased. Wrapped in a spray-on lime-green one-piece, he punches the air with a closed, victorious fist and mock-prays a whispery "thank you" to his nonexistent god.

"Gawd, you look like an old-time superhero!" groans Scrawny from his leather perch at the windowed wall of their NoHio office. Scrawny has visibly lost weight since the two of them opened Chip's file three months ago. He scratches at his left testicle through his own spray-on pants and curses his latest rendezvous in the park.

Ignoring his assistant's comment, King tugs at his own itchy sack and sinks back in his dog-hide chair, into a pose he saves to celebrate each lottery victory.

"Fell for it?"

Scrawny nods, a glint of evil in his eyes before his expression shifts to one of sick curiosity. He clears his throat and asks the question that's been burning his human mind since he began working for King's corp in 2042.

"Ask away," sighs King, reading part of his mind but too lazy to read the rest.

"Why did you start the corp?" Pleased with his cool bravery, Scawny, burdened by youth and tallness, flexes his stiff jaw and waits, barely breathing.

But King doesn't answer him. Instead, he lets his human mind search his memory bank, the part he should've had erased years ago.

The scene is 2014, when spring still arrives in parts of the world. Such as Moronto. He remembers taking the subway home from work on Nay Street, as he always does, to their comfy loft in the heart of the entertainment pit.

The train wheels scrape the tracks and chug its dead-eyed passengers along their monotonous ride of nowhere. King flips open his old cell. ("Get a new phone, Dad. Yours sucks!" his son informs him every day.)

"Call me!" reads his wife's message, the shortest one she's sent all week. He flips his phone closed and does one of those right-hand-absently-scratching-the-left-side-of-the-back-of-the-neck moves. Thinking but not. He sifts through Twiddle Tweets for the rest of his commute.

Two buses and a two-block walk later, he wearily unlocks the condo door and steps inside.

His hyper yellow-haired wife rushes over to him, throws her arms around his neck, drags him aside, and answers his tired confusion before he can speak.

She wiggles her clawed fingers into the back pocket of her suffocating painted-on jeans and produces the little slip of paper that is soon to change everything for them.

Although he's very patient for his unaware age, Scrawny needs his answer.

"Please, King, my shift ends in five minutes."

"Oh god," King mumbles breathlessly. "My third wife won the lottery."

"So sorry to hear that." Scrawny turns his reddening face away from the tired mobster.

The second after Scrawny signs out for the day, King links into his memory and searches for the image that burrows into his human brain every day.

Front page of the *Moronto Moon*. His crystal chandelier. Her body twisted on the ground in a body bag, her arm resting on the blood-sticky pavement beside her, a blob of yellow hair matted and soaked in crimson.

LOTTERY WINNER LOSES LIFE

HOT AND SUNNY
EVERY DAY

Drifting past the sun, a blazing hotness permeates Chip's soul, and this makes him think of her.

"And it'll be sunny and hot *again* today with a high of 50 and, of course, no lows," the weather guy drones on Chip's brain screen.

"It's been this way for months now," drags CoCo with that perfect mix of annoyance and verbal beauty. "Make them reverse this. We can't handle the cancellation of *all* rain!"

"No whining. They want sun." Chip puts on his mean face, an expression creeping over his somewhat delicate features, making them surprisingly hard, dark, and masculine.

Weather guy again. "All I can say is, be careful what you wish for. Sure would be nice to see some rain, any change at all . . ."

They love me for this, muses Chip, pulling a phony pout with his retouched lips and perfectly-groomed 'stache. He grins to reveal a row of disgustingly-perfect chicklets.

"Taxi, sit," he quietly commands the dog from his childhood just because he feels like it. From down the hallway, he swears he sees Taxi sit and pull the infamous fake yawn that all dogs use to tell their masters they'd rather have monkeys throw sand in their eyes. Chip rises to fetch another cup of coffee.

"You disgust me, you and your fucking money!" she roars, grabbing her army jacket from his zebra-skin couch. "You'll make a fabulous future ex-husband."

He sighs and sinks into the matching lazy-girl recliner, puts his feet up, and ponders. The slamming door interrupts his rich thoughts. He stretches out his left hand and touches each fingertip to his palm in a succession of rapid numbers. Staring straight ahead as if seeing something, he opens his mouth.

"Time to change the weather," he purrs in his deepest radio voice. On his brain screen, he can see the man he's speaking to. He pauses while the man says something, and then Chip responds, "Who cares what they want? Things are getting screwed up!" Chip stands now, absently rubbing his right hand on his thigh.

"It's out of our *hands* now," the other voice chuckles. "Should we sink more cash to be a little more persuasive?"

"Too late. People love it this way, hot and sunny every day. *Every day.*"

It isn't long before wildlife begins to die off, crops wither, sleeping volcanoes erupt, earthquakes rumble out of their static states, and Chip tires of wearing shorts every day.

"You *have* to bring rain," he tells his weather contact one day.

"Why? Tourism is at an all-time high since travel agents can guarantee the weather. As long as you stay out of the messed zones, you're all right! Besides, SkinSave sales are through the floor! Have you had pieces of your skin melt off yet? I've heard it's very painful and expensive to replace. SkinSave is the way of the future!"

"Too much of this could lead to world destruction!"

"Yeah, you've got a point. Things are getting out of hand. I'll see what I can do. But you may have to take a cut because of the consequences."

A day later it begins to pour across the globe and doesn't stop for at least forty days and possibly forty nights. As flooding covers the news as a daily event, ruining homes and bringing back the extinct rubber boot, SkinSave reps nervously twitch in their sleep.

It's the only product that promises full protection from the sun. Sprayed on the skin, it works its toxic magic and performs double duty by seeping into the pores and somehow even strengthening the heart and eyeballs, to the point where people develop, yes, x-ray eyes. How amazing to witness someone" heart beating right through their ancient '80s tee.

Un-insurance becomes the norm. Since claims are only allowed when property is damaged because of nonnatural events, such as routine suicide, random public sex, or hovering autos suddenly out of control. Of course, now that weather is finally controlled (with the exception of popular tourism spots such as where Chip lives), there are always messed areas connected to nature. Inner Earth explosions and so on.

Soggy people talk about building arcs but change their minds. The coffee is getting to them, and they can't concentrate long enough to figure out how to use hammers. The world stops thinking while it sits and watches the heavens rain down on them. They take comfort in their Boobies and pray the world will end.

Some turn to various forms of religion—everything from rubbing the Buddha's expanding belly to worshipping traditional torture crosses. Jesus loves them all. But only if they know he does.

Some take comfort in their electronic suicide plans. An exact code tapped from fingertips to palm results in a complete body shutdown of sorts if they choose not to reboot . . . Since PalmTech is invented in 2040, the urge to kill oneself becomes enormously addictive. And the more coffee one drinks, the more creative and urgent the need becomes.

Five years later, suicide is not only accepted but also glorified. It's simply called *exiting*, and those who die up to the challenge are honored and spoken about as if they've become rich massive-mountain climbers.

Trouble comes when hackers get hold of the entire system and begin to shut people down. It's one thing to *choose* to exit, quite another to have someone decide for you. The purpose of shutting people down, of course, is to gain access to their valuable codes and take on new identities, hopefully richer ones. The outdated notion of capitalism is the strongest ever.

Unfortunately, only the rich can afford the antivirus strong enough to block ultimate hacking. Named Code Blue, the chalky substance is injected into the center of the infected palm, therefore flash-freezing the inner connectors, human heart and brain activity, for twenty-four hours. If the victim is lucky, they awake with only an avalanche headache. The less fortunate have their emotions frozen for that lifetime. As a kid, Chip laughs at the thought of robots. At sixty, his stomach flips at the thought.

In the middle of that forty-day downpour, Chip sits witch his CoCo, not contemplating life. They're at a school playground down the street, crouched under a steep slide. They've been playing like kids, tumbling around, swinging high, and leaping off to land shaky legged on the grass and slick around in the muck.

"When will it end?!" she shrieks, delirious and cool to touch, uneven rivers of water streaming down her face, her hair dripping, pouring water over her breasts. He isn't sure if he likes her better this way or when sunlight dances across her bare arms, plays with her chin, pauses on her forehead, creating a permanent halo.

Like a magical force from the skies, that halo glows and spreads over them, beyond them. And the rain stops.

HOT COCO SAVES
THE WORLD

And then floating around in outer space, somewhere between Earth and heaven but definitely closer to heaven and, therefore, closer to his reincarnation or second life, Chip leaves the world to CoCo.

Not realizing Chip has just died in the next room, CoCo uses the end of her pencil to scratch her head where she may have contracted Leopard Lice. She squints through the retro microscope sitting innocently on the table in front of her.

"Beanie!" she shouts, waving her assistant over. A tall gangly apprentice with a shaved head, Beanie strides to her side. He's careful not to touch her.

"Oh my god, look at this," she breathes. "It's like a scene from those early 2000 epidemic movies when the noble vet tries to save the survivors . . . I think I've discovered a cure. Wow, from little old me."

He nods, thinking about her lips, how soft they would be while her mind races ahead to trials, tests, and finally, the end of the palm virus. She's been testing it on chimp hands since, well, since Chip and sidekick invented palming.

Thinking of him now, she waves Beanie away with one dismissive hand and walks down the hall, stares at an unmoving Chip.

"You've lost a lotta blood, darling, as they say in the old movies," she starts then stops, feeling his presence somewhere on the ceiling. She knows he's gone but doesn't regret not taking him to a hospital three months ago when she discovered him on the bloody basement steps. The Win people would've traced him and killed him once he was on public property. Better that he die his own way, having time to concentrate on his second life. She smiles, knowing he'll come out a winner the second time round.

Then just before he fades away permanently from his Chip state, something tugs at his mind. Something in his *Secret SuperBugz* book.

Supposed superbugs have proven to be extremely expensive. SARS sliced nearly $140 billion out of the world economy in the early 2000s, and by the end of the decade, it was discovered the government spent a whopping amount on swine flu vaccines based on old information.

Old information. Ha! He knows what they're up to. Heck, why not throw some hard cash at the next big superbug to appear? He chuckles, and his eyes narrow. Better yet, why not *invent* the next big one? Maybe even disguise it in an everyday addicting beverage. Oh right, he's already done that.

His fading human brain reruns his spend-money list over until he grows bored of it and begins to embellish his lottery dream: become a regular pro at the casino, not caring if he loses; set up his own Snuggle House in a faraway place; cruise around the world in his new yacht; spin around the block in his new go-cart with gold chassis . . .

As the white light beats down on him, dehydrating his soul, his pores crying for water and sense, he continues the delirium: make pizza on a stick and sell it to millions of geese; develop a new poop&scoop bag for fat spiders; convert the money to illegal cash, shred it into confetti, and float it off an overpass to baptize cars . . .

Seven seconds later, his brain aches from all the ideas. Lots and loads of color and speed but no direction, he decides. "Well, it'll be better that way, just spend it on whatever. You don't have to decide right now," he tells himself. At first, his carefree approach is so much fun, so heavenly, so nearly inhuman—just like half his brain.

Bro tries to call him when he's in this state, but he can't palm back. He knows who's palming, can feel the vibrations in his fingers, but dismisses them like flies he wants nothing to do with. "Bro's problem," he tells himself smugly, "is that he drinks too much damn coffee."

As far as he can forget, Bro has a cup of Jim in his hand—not just any cup of Jim—Tom Mortons, maybe even as a kid. Chip is well aware that Bro can't do anything without that cup. He carries it around when he shovels snow, takes it into public washrooms with him, sets it on the nightstand before bedtime, and then sips on the room-temp brew first thing in the morning. That's just to hold him over until he gets his first and best cup of the day. And it's always in those paper mugs, the ones with the damn cat on them.

Hey, when did cats start drinking coffee anyway?

For the last time, Chip relives his first rich year in a blur of slow-motion exhilaration. Weekly trips to the spa, new cars, new clothes, new opportunities to do . . . *nothing* . . . nothing but sit around and have people do things for him. Only him. Trips, ornate elephant knickknacks, real art, drugs, and shoes, new . . . people. And that's all *before* he becomes famous.

"Whatcha doin'?"

She flops down beside him on the couch. His tranced look tells her he's on circle.

"Shhh!" he quips, fingers palming rapidly. "Talkin' to Win."

She sighs and gives him that "not again!" look. He shrugs.

"Sorry, hun, my hands are knotted. Gotta go by their rules. They need me to invest in new tech now. Can you believe it? They think, with my input, they can actually bring back snow!"

Walking out of the room backwards, she lets him go, allowing him to fade from her visuals, his skin melting off his greedy face and dripping to the cast-iron floor, making a steamy puddle between them.

The light in Chip's eyes is bright hot but feels, oh, so good on his aching skin. A tanned smiling host has his arm outstretched in an unexpected traditional handshake. Chip keeps his hands in his pockets. He isn't taking any chances with hackers, especially those who know how to change your whole way of thinking. Best Bud trained him on that one.

The host, his upper lip twitching, withdraws his hand with thundering speed and ad libs the rest.

"Well, now we certainly don't want a lawsuit on our palms, do we?"

"Yeah, I mean, too bad, it's illegal to shake hands these days," counter-chuckles Chip, flipping a flop of red curl out of his eyes once more.

"I *agree*. Just what kind of paranoid, super-germ phobias are we breeding, anyway?" A glint in his eye is Chip's cue to pick up on the comment, take it to its fullest laughable potential.

"You got it. What's a little handshake between friends? Chandler and Joey were fine with it. I mean, is a touch of Ebola gonna scare any of us?"

Shining host thrusts his tanned hands into his own pockets, and the audience laughs back.

"More opportunity for pocket pool," snorts Host, facing the audience and lifting his fingertips inside his black pockets to spread the fabric flat across his groin. "No tight spray-on garb for this guy!" More laughter, this time louder. Of course, Chip takes it to the last level.

"Mine's bigger than yours," he sing-songs, copying Host's erect fingertip show while facing the audience. When the audience has snorted and whistled and cheered itself out, both men, in a clearly-macho manner, clear their throats and sit down, broad, camera-ready grins pasted across their lips.

Chip wants to tell the world about his *Superbugz* book, how he loves to write, how he doesn't give a rat's rump about the damn money. But he doesn't. He just plays along like popular Mr. Rich Guy. His sponsors/enforcers demand it.

It's a loose-knit crew, all the people who control him. Him and his money. His money and, therefore, him. He flashes back to 2011 for a few seconds, recalling the first new hippie protest. For the first time in a long time, people gang together and speak out against corporate greed. In 2020, the riots begin. Now, to the ugly core, he represents the way of life he actually hates. The rich get uglier; the poor get character.

"Let's"—chuckle—"Let's get down to business here"—pause—"Just what was your initial gut reaction when you first found out you actually *won*?"

Chip's stupefied gaze darts from groomed Host to the neutral shag rug beneath his still feet, which are trapped in black dress shoes a size and a half too big. His feet are now captured, exiled to a life of posh pretense. The sofa under his hand is cushy, well-cared for, unlike the tattered, scratchy couch he grows up on, where visions of eating big bowls of Cheerios tangle with the soft hair of a girl.

"Well, naturally, I was in a state of shock," he grunts, his face spreading into rehearsed seriousness.

"Good god, look at his teeth, they actually glow," mumbles a producer as he watches the show backstage on a float screen.

"Guess he can afford it," chuckles his assistant, revealing a row of Boobie-rotted gems.

Chip crosses his black-slacked legs as they do on such shows and brings his hand to his chin in a fake contemplative pose. Sudden hidden horror: He forgot to shave. Not that it matters, as hairless as he is all over his body. CoCo likes that. Says she can feel all his skin, that there's nowhere for it to hide.

When things are big between them in the beginning, they eagerly share their travels, like an extended honeymoon. CoCo fits right into her surroundings wherever she goes . . . in the outdoors. He can see her now, Mount HighEnuff as her backdrop, her face grinning and baring it.

En route to his post-Win vacay, Chip sinks into the narrow seat and closes his eyes, the hum of the plane comforting, an escape from his newly-confusing reality. After a few minutes of bliss, he peers at the woman beside him; she's short, stout, and the ends of her mouth turn down as if she's upset with the world. She senses his peering and produces a sudden smile that transforms her entire face into someone else, her turquoise bauble earrings jiggling with contentment.

She reminds him of Gramma. He took her on a trip once to NoBigDeal, where she promptly drank the water, threw up in the pool, and watched it float all around her as she stood waist-deep in her flowered navy one-piece, simultaneously pale-faced and flushed.

"It's time!" announces Best as Chip approaches heaven.

"Time for what?"

"Time to bring out your own clothing line."

"What?! No way, I'm not even into fashion. Now CoCo, that's a different . . . Can we use her advice?"

"Afraid not. We need a . . . professional who knows how to make a . . . classy image."

"But CoCo could do it. She'd love it. It's right up her field. Wait a minute, are you saying she's not classy?"

Best scratches the back of his head, choosing his next words carefully.

"She's just too . . . creative, that's all. She's too smart for mainstream, and that's exactly what we need to hit with this."

Two weeks later, he visits a designer who takes five hours to come up with the "winning" glove, trouser, and oversized fancy-man hankie.

"You've gotta be kidding!" he spits into the air between them. "Nobody uses hankies anymore. That's just gross!"

"That's just for looks!" she snaps, her straight, angry hair hanging limply around her sharp face.

So there it is, embarrassing actually, a line of clothing with his own Win initials on it. It looks so weird to see LL stitched on something, anything. What does it even mean? Lottery lump? It's all sickeningly pornographic to Chip.

Will a doll be next? He thinks back to when he plays with a Ken doll and shudders. That thing goes through the pond, old Fred's manure pile, atop the shed roof for a year, and finally meets his demise in the chops of Gramps' old hound Chili. No, there will definitely not be a doll. He's putting his hand down on that one.

"Introducing . . . the new Chip doll!" The pouty designer woman waves her stubby hands in animated, conductor-like moves, just a short month later.

"It uh . . . looks just like you," Bro admits to his bro.

Chip blinks and peers at the plastic image of himself—a cross between a skinny wrestler and a phony magician. The hair is a leave-on, although a bit exaggerated, and the face is all off. The real him has way more cheek muscles.

WINNERS ARE LOSERS

What would you do with a gazillion dollars?

I'm just gone—gone fishin'!

At the door of death, Chip's only answer is to live his second life as a homeless person. His identity will be new; nobody will recognize him.

First, he has to say goodbye to the money.

That's the only way he can live his next life in peace. For a second, he shakes his red waves in disbelief and looks himself hard in heaven's cracked mirror.

Then he sees himself resting his ankle against the thin leg of the coffee shop chair. His other foot is flat on the floor, his knee bouncing slightly as if anticipating the end of the world. Across him sits a Win rep, this one long and skinny, expressionless.

"You do realize, Mr. Munk, that giving up the remains of your winnings to *charity* means denial of access to those same winnings . . . for both lifetimes."

A nod, then a clearing of the throat.

"Well, I just need you to sign here to seal the deal."

A smirk.

Chip grabs the pen, waiting patiently in the space between them, pushes away his coffee, then scrawls his initials without reading a word of the contract.

"Does this mean everyone will *finally* be off my back? For good?"

Visions of him running, fleeing to all countries on Earth with Win guys after him, spying on him, following him, too many close texts. On planes . . . who's that guy smirking above his drink? On beaches . . . who's following him at night in the silent sands? Then ultimate face-to-face encounters, an elderly man grabbing him in an airport but he breaks free. A librarian scolds him for overdue books then puts his palm in his own pocket . . . searching for a Taser?

A nod, quick and efficient.

"You're a free man, Chip Munk. Would you like the memory base of your lottery winnings erased?"

Chip shakes his head slowly.

"No. I need reminding of certain life lessons here."

"Good man."

And with that, the meeting is done, and the money is on its way to the government, where it is rapidly used to gain control of future lottery winners.

In the meantime, the animals begin their takeover. This is no *Planet of the Apes*! It's a real showdown, and CoCo feels it coming in the middle of one night when a niggling, far-fetched dream catches the attention of her side-conscious. All they have to do is walk in, unplug the humans from their PalmTech, spin them around by their coffee-swelling brains, and send them on their way like a creaky arc in a giant storm.

HOMELESS HOME

Following a deafening crack of light, Chip finds himself in his new body, in his new life, sitting on the curb, knees turned in, arms crossed. He looks down at his skinny arms and legs, the limbs of a malnourished teen, unwashed and unfed. He feels very Oliver Twisty, a foreign pain in his stomach radiating out to each limb and to the center of his human brain.

So this is how it works. For your second life, you're zapped into a different body and somehow shuttled to Earth. Like a bad sci-fi rerun. No time to waste on simply being born again.

Chip watches his life plan begin to unpeel immediately.

The homeless thing just had to start on the coldest day of the month.

He can't *believe* how damn cold it is. Most of his fingers feel gone. He knows a hacker would have to work really hard to saw through his frozen wrists. The blood wouldn't gush and spurt; it would just cling sluggishly to the outer walls of his veins. He chuckles at his former whining self who could barely get from parking lot to bank without cursing winter air.

Then it was frosty; now it's biting, searing through his flesh until he imagines his fingers replaced with frozen stubs. His breath fogs out behind him, something he'd once notice with a shrug and note of whimsy, now replaced with the heavy insult of survival, his nostrils sticking together for a few seconds with each intake.

It's never this cold anymore. It never snows. Over the decade, GW (global warming) and WC (weather control) prove to be king, and people get sun-fried in January for Satan's sake. Sledding becomes grass sliding, snowmen cry . . . An organization called SnowWeepers sweeps the nation with its pray-for-snow meetings and tears-for-toboggans tea parties.

Chip pushes the door open, and a wall of heat shocks his frozen face, stings it back to present day.

"Hey," greets a self-amused teen slumped behind the counter. "So this is snow! Cold out there. Need anything?" He winks.

Where? Where is the goddamn snow?

Counter Boy is wearing a plaid shirt from the '80s. There's a zombie prep book in his hand. Despite the thick beard covering half his face and most of his expression, he looks dejected when Chip shrugs.

"Be great if we could all win the *lottery*," Counter Boy chuckles, giving a pathetic once-over and half-searching Chip's too-radiant smile.

"No, thanks," Chip beams. "Just need a minute to warm up, thanks."

After twenty minutes of slowly rubbing his wind-chapped hands, he can feel his veins waking up, the blood flowing strong. The burned red has already disappeared from his cheeks, a seasoned gleam never leaving his pale eyes. As he turns to leave, the cashier tosses him a pair of dusty gloves from behind the counter.

"Here—these things are so old they'll never sell. I think they're from back in the day when the world was saved by some vet or something and everything went back to the basics. They're yours, darlin'. Let me know when it's not a girls-night-in, and we'll party."

Chip shudders and pulls on the gloves. They're stiff, lined with crusty felt, far too large for her skinny hands. The initials LL are stitched on the palms.

Printed in the United States
by Baker & Taylor Publisher Services